Rhymes
to Count On

Compiled by Judy Nayer
Pictures by Louise Bates

© 1990 McClanahan Book Company, Inc. All rights reserved.
Published by McClanahan Book Company, Inc.
23 West 26th Street, New York, NY 10010
PRINTED IN THE UNITED STATES OF AMERICA
ISBN 1-56293-104-0

Two little blackbirds sitting on a hill,
One named Jack, the other named Jill.
Fly away, Jack! Fly away, Jill!
Come back, Jack! Come back, Jill!

One, two, three, four, five,
I caught a fish alive.
Six, seven, eight, nine, ten,
I let it go again.

Why did you let it go?
Because it bit my finger so.
Which finger did it bite?
The little finger on the right.

One potato, two potato,
Three potato, four,
Five potato, six potato,
Seven potato, MORE!

One little, two little,
Three little Indians;
Four little, five little,
Six little Indians;
Seven little, eight little,
Nine little Indians;
Ten little Indian boys.

One, two,
Buckle my shoe;

Three, four,
Knock at the door;

Five, six,
Pick up sticks;

Seven, eight,
Lay them straight;

Nine, ten,
A big fat hen;

Eleven, twelve,
Dig and delve;

Thirteen, fourteen,
Maids a-courting;

Fifteen, sixteen,
Maids in the kitchen;

Seventeen, eighteen,
Maids a-waiting;

Nineteen, twenty,
My plate's empty.

One, two, three and four,
Mary's at the cottage door.
Five, six, seven, eight,
Eating cherries off a plate.

Chook, chook, chook, chook, chook,
Good morning, Mrs. Hen.
How many chickens have you got?
Madam, I've got ten.
Four of them are yellow,
And four of them are brown,
And two of them are speckled red,
The nicest in the town.

Three young rats with black felt hats,
Three young ducks with white straw flats,
Three young dogs with curling tails,
Three young cats with demi-veils,
Went out to walk with two young pigs
In satin vests and sorrel wigs.

But suddenly it chanced to rain
And so they all went home again.

This Old Man

This old man, he played one,
He played knick-knack on my drum.
With a knick-knack, paddy whack,
    give the dog a bone,
This old man came rolling home.

This old man, he played two,
He played knick-knack on my shoe.
With a knick-knack, paddy whack,
    give the dog a bone,
This old man came rolling home.

This old man, he played three,
He played knick-knack on my knee.
With a knick-knack, paddy whack,
   give the dog a bone,
This old man came rolling home.

This old man, he played four,
He played knick-knack on my door.
With a knick-knack, paddy whack,
   give the dog a bone,
This old man came rolling home.

This old man, he played five,
He played knick-knack on a hive.
With a knick-knack, paddy whack,
   give the dog a bone,
This old man came rolling home.

This old man, he played six,
He played knick-knack on my sticks.
With a knick-knack, paddy whack,
    give the dog a bone,
This old man came rolling home.

This old man, he played seven,
He played knick-knack up to heaven.
With a knick-knack, paddy whack,
    give the dog a bone,
This old man came rolling home.

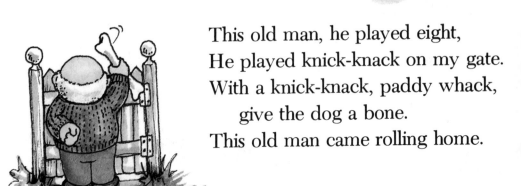

This old man, he played eight,
He played knick-knack on my gate.
With a knick-knack, paddy whack,
    give the dog a bone.
This old man came rolling home.

This old man, he played nine,
He played knick-knack on my line.
With a knick-knack, paddy whack,
    give the dog a bone,
This old man came rolling home.

This old man, he played ten,
He played knick-knack over again.
With a knick-knack, paddy whack,
    give the dog a bone,
This old man came rolling home.

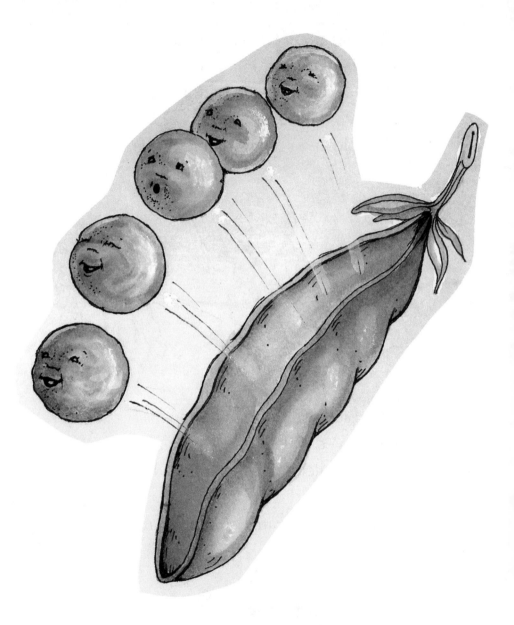

Five little peas in a pea pod pressed,
One grew, two grew, and so did all the rest.
They grew and grew and they did not stop,
Until all of a sudden the pod went *pop*!

Grandma's baked a cake for me.
See the candles, one, two, three.
Put them out with one big blow.
Ready, set, now here we go.

Ten little bluebirds perched on a pine,
One flew away and then there were nine.

Nine little bluebirds sitting up late,
One flew away and then there were eight.

Eight little bluebirds looking high to heaven,
One flew away and then there were seven.

Seven little bluebirds picking up sticks,
One flew away and then there were six.

Six little bluebirds glad to be alive,
One flew away and then there were five.

Five little bluebirds sitting on a door,
One flew away and then there were four.

Four little bluebirds singing merrily,
One flew away and then there were three.

Three litle bluebirds hidden in a shoe,
One flew away and then there were two.

Two little bluebirds pecking at a crumb,
One flew away and then there was one.

One little bluebird chirping in the sun,
It flew away and then there were none.

There Were Ten in the Bed

There were ten in the bed,
And the little one said,
Roll over, roll over.
So they all rolled over,
And one fell out.

There were nine in the bed,
And the little one said,
Roll over, roll over.
So they all rolled over,
And one fell out.

There were eight in the bed,
And the little one said,
Roll over, roll over.
So they all rolled over,
And one fell out.

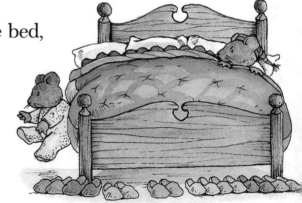

There were seven in the bed,
And the little one said,
Roll over, roll over.
So they all rolled over,
And one fell out.

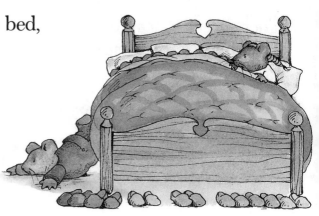

There were six in the bed,
And the little one said,
Roll over, roll over.
So they all rolled over,
And one fell out.

There were five in the bed,
And the little one said,
Roll over, roll over.
So they all rolled over,
And one fell out.

There were four in the bed,
And the little one said,
Roll over, roll over.
So they all rolled over,
And one fell out.

There were three in the bed,
And the little one said,
Roll over, roll over.
So they all rolled over,
And one fell out.

There were two on the bed,
And the little one said,
Roll over, roll over.
So they all rolled over,
And one fell out.

There was one in the bed,
And he said,
Roll over, roll over.
So he rolled over,
And he fell out,
There were none in the bed,
So nobody said,
Roll over, roll over.

Four corners to my bed,
Four angels round my head,
One to read and one to write,
Two to guard my bed at night.